SONA SHARMA

A FRIEND INDEED

CHITRA SOUNDAR

Illustrated by JEN KHATUN

WALKER
BOOKS

TO ALL FRIENDS WHO FIGHT FOR FAIR ELECTIONS

First published in Great Britain 2022 by Walker Books Ltd
87 Vauxhall Walk, London SE11 5HJ

2 4 6 8 10 9 7 5 3 1

Text © 2022 Chitra Soundar
Illustrations © 2022 Jen Khatun

This book has been typeset in Alegreya

Printed and bound by CPI Group (UK) Ltd, Croydon CR0 4YY

British Library Cataloguing in Publication Data:
a catalogue record for this book is available from the British Library

ISBN 978-1-5295-0438-5

www.walker.co.uk

CONTENTS

Exciting News?

Sona Sharma lives in a large joint family full of happy people who argue sometimes. Relatives come unannounced, the phone rings often and everyone is always welcome whatever the time.

These are Sona's people:

Amma – Sona's mum.

She is a music teacher and singer. She's always humming a song or listening to music.

Appa – Sona's dad. He works with computers all day and sometimes at night too.

Minmini – Minmini means "firefly" and she is Sona's baby sister, who is almost one.

Thatha – Sona's grandfather. He knows a lot of things. And when he doesn't know about something, he tells a story about something else.

Paatti – Sona's grandmother. She makes the best sweets in the

whole world. She always
laughs at Thatha's jokes.

The President – Sona's
other grandmother. Sona
doesn't know her real name.
The President used to be the
president of some college, so
everyone calls her that still. She lives in the
only orange house in the entire neighbourhood,
called The Orange.

Joy and Renu – Sona's friends from school.
They live a street away and go to school with
Sona in an auto-rickshaw.

Mullai – Sona's auto-rickshaw driver. She
picks up Sona, Joy and Renu in that order, to
drop off at school. In the evening she takes
them home – Renu first, Joy next and Sona last.
She's never late and
recites a lot of
Tamil poetry.

Elephant – Sona's best friend. He fits perfectly in her toy bag and her cuddly chair and next to her on her pillow. Sona never goes anywhere without him, except, of course, to school.

It was Monday morning and the beginning of a new week. Sona said goodbye to Elephant and went downstairs with her school bag.

HONK!

Mullai, her auto-rickshaw driver, had arrived to pick up Sona for school.

"Bye!" she shouted to Thatha, hurrying to get into the auto-rickshaw.

"You seem very excited to get to school today," said Mullai. She started the auto-rickshaw with a loud *FUT-FUT-FUT* and they were off.

"Miss Rao said she has something special to announce today," said Sona. "I can't wait to find out what it is."

Joy and Renu were excited too.

"Maybe Miss Rao is getting married," said Joy.

"Ooh! Will she invite us to the wedding?" asked Renu.

When they reached school, Miss Rao was getting ready for the day, humming a song to herself.

"What is the exciting thing, Miss?" asked Sona.

"Good morning to you too, Sona," said Miss Rao.

"Good morning, Miss Rao," all three of them chorused dutifully.

"Please tell us about the exciting news!" Sona prompted.

"Not yet," said Miss Rao. "After we mark the attendance register."

Sona groaned. Marking the register took a long time in their class. When Miss Rao called a name, that person had to reply back with a fact instead of simply saying "Present". Miss Rao would choose the type of facts each day. They had already covered extinct animals, rivers of the world and Indian scientists.

"Let's list states of India today," said Miss Rao.

After all the names were ticked off, Miss Rao closed the register and said, "So..."

She was going to tell them the exciting news. *Please, please, let it be a field trip*, thought Sona, grinning at Renu and Joy.

"... you all know that every class must have a class leader," said Miss Rao.

Everyone nodded.

"Usually, teachers pick someone who has demonstrated leadership," continued Miss Rao.

"How do you demon—stra—te leadership?" asked Joy.

13

"I'm a leader," said Pradeep. Pradeep had transferred from another city to their school the year before. Ever since he'd got there, he was always boasting about himself.

"Shh!" said Miss Rao. "But this time I'm not going to pick someone."

"Then we don't get a class leader?" asked Sona.

"You're all going to elect a leader in an election," said Miss Rao. "Isn't that exciting?"

An election? Sona had always thought elections were for grown-ups and definitely not exciting.

"Can children vote in elections?" she asked.

"This is our class election," said Miss Rao, "and so you will be voting."

"Will you be voting, Miss?" asked Renu.

"No, I will be the Election Commissioner,"

said Miss Rao. "That means I make the rules and ensure that the election is conducted properly."

"Who will we vote for?" asked Sona.

"We will have candidates," said Miss Rao. "Who can tell me what the word 'candidate' means?"

"A candidate is candy made of dates," said Joy, giggling, "and we can pick the one we like."

Everyone laughed. Even Miss Rao. "Good wordplay, Joy," she said, turning to the whiteboard. She wrote the word "candidate" with a blue pen and turned back to the class.

"A candidate is someone who wants to become the class leader," said Miss Rao. "If there is more than one candidate, then we need an election to see who gets the most votes."

"So, we don't need an election, Miss," said Pradeep. "Everyone will choose me."

"Can anyone become a class leader as long as they win the election?" asked Joy.

"That's right," said Miss Rao. "As long as you become a candidate and get the most votes."

Miss Rao explained that each person in the class would need to think about who to vote for because whoever they chose would be their class leader for the entire year.

"What if we don't like any of the candidates?" someone else asked.

"Then you can abstain," said Miss Rao, writing the word on the board. "That means you decide not to vote. But I hope none of you will abstain because our class surely has very good candidates."

"Everyone will vote for me," said Pradeep. Again!

Renu groaned loudly. Joy rolled her eyes at Pradeep. Sona decided she must do something

about Pradeep's boasting. She didn't want the entire class abstaining. She definitely did not want Pradeep to be their class leader for an entire year.

"Well, you're not the only candidate any more, are you?" said Sona. "Miss, I want to be a candidate too."

Some of the girls clapped. Pradeep stuck out his tongue at her.

Miss Rao smiled. "Good, we're getting started. We have two candidates now."

Sona turned towards Joy and Renu triumphantly. But Joy wasn't smiling.

Neither was Renu. The rest of the day was filled with discussions about elections. In Geography, Miss Rao showed them the symbols of famous political parties across India. In Maths, they drew bar graphs of election results. In English, they learned the meanings of words related to elections and how to spell them.

"Isn't 'constituency' the hardest word ever?" Sona turned to Joy and asked.

But Joy didn't reply. Before Sona could ask about it, the bell rang and it was break time. Joy and Renu ran away together.

At first, Sona didn't think much of it. She decided to talk to them during lunch. But at lunch, when Joy and Renu sat on their own under the neem tree, far away from her, Sona's eyes filled up with tears.

This was the first time she had ever eaten lunch on her own. Even Paatti's vermicelli upma didn't taste good with tears. But she didn't want to cry in front of her classmates. What if they thought she wasn't a good candidate? Sona finished her lunch and went to the library to read *The Big Book of Bad Dad Jokes*. Appa always said funny books are great for sad times.

INVITING TROUBLE

The rest of the day was just like the morning. Miss Rao talked about elections. Joy and Renu didn't talk to Sona at all.

That evening, when they got into the rickshaw, Mullai immediately knew something was wrong. "What's going on?" she asked. "Did Miss Rao resign from the school or something?"

"No," whispered Sona.

"Then what?" asked Mullai.

No one said anything. Before Mullai could ask them any more questions, cars and bikes started honking behind her. As Mullai swerved into the busy road, Sona nudged Joy. "Why are you both not talking to me?" she asked.

Joy just shook her head and turned away. Renu pretended she didn't hear.

"It's not fair if you don't tell me," said Sona.

But they didn't reply. Nor did they say goodbye when Mullai dropped them off at their homes.

"Sona, what's wrong?" asked Mullai one more time as Sona got off. Sona just shook her head. "Talk to someone," said Mullai. "A problem shared is a problem halved."

Sona wanted to talk to someone about what had happened at school. But when she walked inside the house, everyone in her family was busy.

Paatti was writing a list of groceries. "Sorry, Sona," she said, not even looking up. "I've left a plate with snacks for you in the kitchen."

Amma was talking to the tailor on her phone. "Yes, we want them measured and stitched. But can you deliver them by Friday night, please?"

Thatha was talking to the motorbike priest. "Yes, yes, I'll get all the stuff for the ceremony."

On a normal day, Sona wouldn't have minded so much. But today was definitely not a normal day. Sona couldn't stop her tears any longer. She went up to her room and hugged Elephant close and sobbed.

"What's wrong?" asked Elephant.

"Joy and Renu stopped speaking to me and I don't know why and I'm running for class leader and ... and..."

"And what?"

"Everyone's busy downstairs," said Sona, sniffing. "It's like someone pressed the rewind button and we have

gone back to Minmini's naming ceremony when
no one had time for me."

Elephant hugged Sona tightly back.
Sometimes Sona just needed him to listen.
Even if he couldn't fix the things that had gone
wrong.

"Knock knock," said Amma from the other
side of the door.

Sona was quiet.

"You're supposed to say, 'Who's there?',"

prompted Elephant.

"Knock knock,"
said Amma again.
Minmini giggled.

Elephant nudged
Sona. "Your turn,"
he said.

"Who's there?"
Sona whispered,
wiping her face on
her sleeve.

"Mummy!" said

Amma in a muffled voice.

"Mummy who?" asked Sona with a giggle.

"A mummy who's alive!" shouted Amma as she opened the door and walked in pretending to be an Egyptian mummy carrying a laughing baby.

"Don't be silly, Amma," said Sona.

Amma put Minmini on the bed and sat next to Sona. "What's wrong?" she said. "Are you not feeling well?"

"I'm OK," said Sona.

"If you want to talk..." said Amma.

"No!"

"OK, then, get ready, change into a silk top and skirt," said Amma. "We're going to invite our neighbours and friends."

"Invite them for what?" asked Sona.

"This Saturday is Minmini's first birthday, according to our Tamil calendar," said Amma. "We'll perform the Ayush Homam ceremony, to wish her a long and healthy life."

"Oh," whispered Sona. She should have guessed. It was always about Minmini.

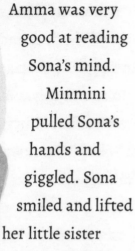

"We did one for you too," said Amma. Amma was very good at reading Sona's mind. Minmini pulled Sona's hands and giggled. Sona smiled and lifted her little sister gently up onto her lap.

"Advance happy birthday, little firefly," said Sona. She had promised to be the best big sister ever and she wasn't going to forget that. "Shall I wear the red skirt, Amma?"

"Great!" said Amma. "See you downstairs in ten minutes!"

"Can I bring Elephant?" asked Sona.

"Yes, of course," said Amma.

Sona got ready quickly and went downstairs with Elephant. "It's good you stopped crying and you're doing something nice for Minmini," said Elephant.

"That's how big sisters are," replied Sona.

Amma was packing a big stack of invitations into a cloth bag and holding a little silver kumkuma chimizh with tiny silver bells that contained vermilion.

Paatti came over to them and said, "Don't forget to invite Sona's friends. She *is* the big sister, after all."

"We'll go to Joy's house first," said Amma, walking ahead.

Sona stood frozen at the door. She didn't want to go to Joy's house. Not today.

"Come on, Sona," called Amma.

"Didn't you want to be the best big sister?" Elephant reminded her.

Sona nodded. Elephant was right. She must do this for Minmini even if it made her sad. Sona followed Amma with a big smile on her face. But Elephant was sure that her smile didn't reach her eyes.

At Joy's house, Sona stood behind Amma clutching Elephant, rather than rushing to Joy to hug and dance, like she normally did.

"Hello, Joy!" said Amma, handing a yellow invitation to Joy's mum and said, "Everyone must come and bless Minmini."

"Of course," said Joy's mum. "We'll be there."

"I won't," spluttered Joy and she ran inside.

Amma laughed. But it wasn't her happy laugh.

It was her I'm-not-sure-this-is-fun laugh, like when Appa played pranks on her.

"Sona, did you and Joy have a fight at school?" asked Amma.

Sona shook her head.

"Well, I'm sure they'll sort it out tomorrow," said Joy's mum. "Let's not blow it up and make it bigger. See you on Saturday."

On their way to another neighbour's house, Amma asked again, "Did you have a fight with Joy?"

Sona shook her head. "She just suddenly stopped talking to me," said Sona. "Renu too."

"Should we go to Renu's house now and ask why?" asked Amma.

"No!" said Sona, a bit louder than she meant to.

"If you want to talk," said Amma, "you know I'm here."

"Me too," said Elephant.

Sona nodded as she hugged Elephant tight.

When they got home, she disappeared upstairs with Elephant, claiming she had homework.

"Do you really have homework?" asked Elephant.

"No," said Sona, picking up a book to read, and

then closing it. She opened her drawing book, and then closed it.

Elephant tried to cheer Sona up by falling from the desk. But Sona didn't laugh or pick him up. She left Elephant quiet on the floor as she turned her puzzle cube over and over again in her hands. *Click-click-click!*

CAT AND MICE

On Tuesday morning, when Miss Rao had finished the register (that day it was names of colours), Joy got up and said, "Miss, I want to be a candidate too!"

"That's wonderful, Joy," said Miss Rao.

What?! Why would Joy become a candidate? Shouldn't she be helping Sona win? They were best friends, after all, thought Sona.

"Any change of heart from you two – Pradeep and Sona?" asked Miss Rao. "Are you still in the running?"

"Yes, Miss," said Pradeep.

I was the one who stood up against Pradeep first, thought Sona. *I won't drop out.* "Yes, Miss," she said. "I'm still a candidate."

"All right," said Miss Rao. "We have three candidates and it's going to be an exciting election."

Miss Rao was wrong, thought Sona. Exciting things happened only when she was with her friends. Not when she was fighting with them. Perhaps if she explained to Joy that she *had* to win to beat Pradeep, maybe Joy would drop out.

"Joy!" called Sona. "I want to talk to you."

Joy didn't turn around.

"Please!" said Sona.

"What?" barked Joy.

"Why did you become a

candidate?" Sona asked. "Perhaps we should have talked about it?"

"Then why didn't you talk about it before you stood up in class?" asked Renu.

Oh! But she had to stop Pradeep, hadn't she? "No ... but ..." she said, "I didn't want Pradeep to become the class leader."

"But do *you* want to be the class leader?" asked Joy.

Sona wasn't sure about that. She didn't reply.

"I really want to be class leader," said Joy, "and that's why I'm a candidate."

Even though they were fighting, Sona knew that Joy would be a great class leader. She'd never jump into things without thinking, like Sona did. But now there was nothing else to do but fight against her own best friend.

That evening, when Sona went home, she was relieved that no one was paying any attention to her. They were all busy with the preparations for Saturday. Even the President.

Sona decided to discuss her election troubles with Elephant and Minmini. They always helped her find the right way to do things.

Minmini was in her playpen next to Appa, who was working with his headphones on. When Sona came in with Elephant, Appa signalled that he was on the phone.

Sona sat next to Minmini with Elephant.

"What's wrong?" asked Elephant. "You seem a bit upset. No, you're—"

"Angry," said Sona.

Minmini touched Sona's face. Sona smiled.

"Joy is a candidate too now," explained Sona. "We're both competing against Pradeep."

"I'm so happy elephants don't have elections," said Elephant.

Minmini said, "Mmm."

"Elephant elections are fights," said Sona.

"Oh!" said Elephant. "What are you actually worried about – fighting with Joy?"

"No, I'm worried that Pradeep will win because Joy and I are busy fighting against each other."

"That's exactly like the story of the cat and the two mice," said Appa. He must have finished his call and was listening.

He removed his headphones and said, "It's one of Paatti's stories that Thatha told me."

Sona loved stories. But she couldn't remember the last time Appa had told her one.

"Please can you tell us the story?" she asked. "Minmini wants to hear it too."

37

"Oh, right!" said Appa. "Sure, why not. I won't do as good a job as Thatha, but I'll try. This is a story about appam."

"You mean aapam?"

"No, aapam is a pancake with coconut milk," said Appa. "An appam is a sweet that Paatti makes for special festivals. They are round and deep-fried in oil."

"Yum!" said Sona.

Appa began the story.

Once upon a time, two mice – Yeli and Meli – lived in the garden of a big house. One day Yeli spotted a big appam in the kitchen. Meli dragged it out.

But they couldn't agree on sharing the treat.

"I should get a bigger share because I found it," said Yeli.

"I should get a bigger share because I brought it out," said Meli.

Vida, the hungry cat, was watching them. He wanted to eat the appam too. "Shall I divide it for you?" Vida offered.

Yeli and Meli agreed because they didn't trust each other.

Vida tore the appam into two pieces. One piece was bigger than the other.

"Make it equal," said Yeli.

Vida chewed on the big piece to make it smaller.

"Now this piece is bigger," said Meli. "Make it equal."

So Vida chewed on the other piece to make it smaller.

This went on and on until there were only two tiny pieces of appam left.

"Uh-oh!" said Yeli. "You've eaten almost all the appam."

"You cheated us!" said Meli.

"If you don't scoot now, I'll eat you both up right after I finish eating," growled Vida.

Yeli and Meli scampered back into their burrow as Vida said with a grin, "The cat gets a bite when the mice begin to fight!"

"The end," said Appa, and made an evil cat face and meowed loudly. That made Minmini and Sona giggle.

"Thank you for telling me the story," said Sona.

"You're welcome," replied Appa. "If you want to talk about it, I'm always here to listen."

"...Then you and Joy must work together, right?" asked Elephant.

"Yes, we must work together to make sure *I* win," said Sona.

"Maybe Joy and Renu should listen to the story too," said Elephant.

But Joy and Renu wouldn't even look at her, let alone listen. Maybe she could draw the story, she thought. As Sona started to draw, Elephant wondered if appam tasted like coconuts or bananas.

Wednesday

- Election laws discussion
- lunch
- Art class

FAIR ELECTIONS

It was Wednesday morning. Just two days to go before the class leader election.

"Class, listen up!" Miss Rao began. "Elections must be conducted fairly. Therefore, I've created rules for our candidates – Pradeep, Sona and Joy. If the candidate or their friends break any of the rules, that candidate will be disqualified."

43

ELECTION LAWS

1. You can put up posters only inside our classroom.

2. No name-calling, bad language or insults.

3. No fake news.

4. No promises you cannot keep.

5. Do not harass the voters.

"What are the rules?" asked Renu.

Miss Rao put up a poster on their classroom wall.

"Please can you explain what 'No fake news' means?" asked Joy.

"You mustn't spread lies about Pradeep or Sona," said Miss Rao. "Like saying, 'Sona turns into a dragon at night'. Or, 'Pradeep ate snakes for breakfast'."

The class broke out into giggles as Pradeep pretended to eat snakes.

"Don't make promises that you cannot keep," said Miss Rao. "For example, don't say, 'I'll get you extra time in our tests', because you're not the teacher."

Sona, Pradeep and Joy nodded.

"Who knows what 'harass' means?" asked Miss Rao.

No one said anything.

"It means bothering someone for votes," continued Miss Rao. "Like when they are reading quietly in the library or washing their hands in the bathroom."

"Can I ask for votes when we are standing in line for assembly?" asked Pradeep.

"Are you allowed to talk when you're standing in line?" asked Miss Rao.

"No," said Sona.

"Then no," said Miss Rao.

Pradeep groaned loudly.

Just this once, Sona agreed with Pradeep. How were they going to get any votes if they couldn't ask anyone for them? Joy must have been thinking the same thing. She stood up and said, "Miss, maybe there should be a special time for asking for votes."

Miss Rao tapped her pencil on her forehead

for a few seconds. That usually meant
she was thinking. Then she said,
"That's a fair request. You can
have one period tomorrow for
election work."

Miss Rao continued,
"On Friday morning, the
candidates will get five
minutes each to make
a speech in front of the
class."

Joy and Renu high-
fived. Sona felt left out.

It was not until lunchtime
that Sona remembered the
Cat and Mice comic book. When Renu went to
the toilet, Sona followed her. "Hey, Renu," she
called. "I brought you this."

"What is it?" asked Renu.

"It's a comic book I made," said Sona. "See,
you can unfold it like this to read the whole
story."

"You're not allowed to harass me in the toilet," said Renu. "Remember what Miss Rao said."

"But I'm not harassing you," said Sona. "I just thought you might like to read my story. You always do."

"I'm busy," said Renu.

Sona returned to the classroom and put the comic book back in her bag. Sona wouldn't win if she had to fight against Joy in the election. She *had* to persuade Joy to drop out. But how was Joy going to understand that if she didn't read the story?

Miss Rao looked up from her desk. "Sona! Go and eat your lunch. Otherwise you'll be late for Art class."

Art class. That gave Sona an idea.

In Art class Mrs Ghani let them make a lot of mess. There were paints, clay for pottery, paper cut-outs, a green screen for taking photos – it was a place where Sona was really happy, even if Elephant was never there. There was also a giant pin-up board where everyone could display their artwork.

When Sona showed Mrs Ghani her comic book, Mrs Ghani clapped her hands and said, "Wonderful! Very creative. I'm going to put it up on the board for everyone to see."

Sona's plan had worked. It was right there for everyone to see – even Joy and Renu.

"We're going to do a collage about elections," said Mrs Ghani. And she began to give them ideas on what to do.

Sona was busy on her own, cutting and sticking pictures, but she looked up often to see if anyone was reading her story.

"It's almost time," said Mrs Ghani. "Put away your projects, throw the rubbish into the right bins and wash your hands."

Renu wandered over to the board, on her way to the bins. Then Joy went to the board too.

This is my chance, thought Sona, as she hurried over. "I made the comic book," she said.

"Yeah, we know," said Renu.

"Appa told me that story to show me that if we fight each other, Pradeep will win the election," said Sona. "See, Pradeep is the cat."

Joy looked at Sona's drawing of the cat and smiled a little. Then she put her frown back on.

"So what?" asked Renu.

"Maybe if Joy dropped out," said Sona, "then I could get more votes than Pradeep."

Joy turned around to look at Sona. "Maybe if you drop out," said Joy, "I can beat Pradeep. Did you even think about that?"

Sona's eyes filled with tears. Why was Joy twisting and turning everything she said? Sona had become a candidate before Joy had even thought about it. Why should *she* drop out?

SONA THE
PARTY PLANNER

That evening, when Sona returned home from
school, the grown-ups were having a meeting at
the dining table, with a tumbler of coffee each.

"We're waiting for you," said Amma.

"Why?" asked Sona. Her legs trembled a little.
Had they found out about her fight with Joy and
Renu?

"You're awfully quiet," said Thatha. "You're not bursting with news from school."

Uh-oh! Had Miss Rao called home?

"Wash up and come down, Sona," said Paatti. "I've made your favourite tiffin."

"Please can I have some too?" asked Appa. "Or is it reserved only for granddaughters?"

Sona ran upstairs without saying a word.

"What's going on?" she asked Elephant.

"I don't know," said Elephant. "No one tells me anything. Except you."

Sona was hungry. She had to go down to get her tiffin. Even if that meant they were going to make her talk about things she didn't want to talk about.

When Sona went downstairs with Elephant, everyone went quiet.

"Maybe they were talking about us," said Elephant.

"Here, Sona," said Paatti, handing her a plate with steaming idlies and a cup of red tomato chutney. And she handed a plate to Appa too.

"Thanks, Paatti," said Sona, tearing a piece of idli and dipping it into the cup of chutney.

"Ask them," said Elephant.

"Why were you waiting for me?" asked Sona.

"It's about Saturday's ceremony, sweetie," said Amma. "The grown-ups are going to be doing the homam – the chanting and the prayers. Thatha thinks the kids will need entertainment, away from the smoke."

"What smoke?" asked Sona.

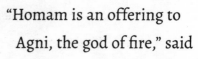

"Homam is an offering to Agni, the god of fire," said Thatha. "That means we will light a small fire, and add ghee and rice into it, which often causes smoke to rise."

"Hmmph!" grunted the President. "Children nowadays... When we were little, we didn't mind it at all because the smoke was good for you."

Elephant wasn't sure smoke was good. In the forest, if there was smoke, elephants always ran away as fast as they could.

"Anyway, I thought," said Thatha, "maybe you and Joy and Renu could put on a show like you do in the summer holidays?"

Sona almost hiccupped on her idli.

"Eat slowly," said Paatti. "Hurry brings worry."

"Great idea, right?" said Appa.

"Sorry!" shouted Sona, a bit louder than she wanted to. "You know I'm running for class leader in our class elections."

"Yes, but that'll be over by Friday evening, right?" asked Amma.

"Yeah, but I won't have time to do any planning until then," said Sona.

"Well, that's perfect," said Amma. "I'll ask Joy and Renu's parents to send them here for breakfast on Saturday. Then you'll have all morning to plan and plot."

Sona wasn't sure if Amma was trying to help her patch up her fight with Joy and Renu or if they were just worried about having a fun birthday for Minmini.

"No, thanks," said Sona. "I don't want to do a show with Joy and Renu. OK?"

"But why?" asked Appa. "Is this because you're competing against Joy in the election?"

Everyone gasped. Even the President.

Sona thought all their gasps were like big fat fingers of blame pointing at her. She couldn't

hold in her tears any more. Amma rushed to Sona's side quickly and pulled her into a cuddle.

"Hey! It's OK to compete against your friend," said Amma. "It's just like sports day, right?"

Sona shook her head as she sobbed. "It's not," she yelled, squashing Elephant into her chest as she cried into Amma's sari.

"Oh dear," said the President. "It seems Sona wants to win and Joy wants to win too! It's a battle between buddies. The worst kind of battle."

"Mum!" said Amma. "It's not a battle. It's just a class election."

"And Sona is going to win," said Appa, coming over to give Sona a sandwich cuddle.

"Yes she is," said Paatti. She pulled in Thatha and they all did a bonda cuddle, which was a cuddle from all sides.

And then, as if she sensed Sona's sadness, Minmini started to cry.

"Uh-oh!" said Appa. "Minmini wants to join in the cuddle too."

"Please no," cried Elephant. "I'm already squished!"

"I'll get Minmini," said the President, whistling to Minmini as she picked her up from the playpen. Minmini loved whistles, just as much as Sona loved ... tickles.

Of course, Amma knew that. She tickled Sona. Sona's sobs turned into giggles. "Stop!" she cried between giggles.

The bonda cuddle turned into tickle-wriggle and soon everyone was laughing and giggling.

Finally, when the last of the giggles was gone, Sona sat quietly, hugging Elephant.

"Why didn't you tell us anything until now?" asked Paatti.

"You were all busy with the first-birthday ceremony," said Sona.

"I see," said Amma. "We're sorry we didn't pay attention. Sometimes grown-ups are so busy with their own plans that they forget to notice important things. Please tell us now and we'll try our best to help you."

Elephant nudged Sona. "Tell them," he said.

Sona wasn't sure how they could help, but she couldn't stop her words any more. They tumbled out like a waterfall in the forest, jumping down a hill. She told them everything, right up to the comic book story and what Joy had said.

"You made a comic book from my story?" asked Appa. "Incredible!"

"My story," said Thatha.

"My story, actually," said Paatti.

Amma raised her hand like a traffic policeman. "That's not important, is it?" she asked in a stern voice, that sounded just like the President. "So much has been going on and we didn't notice," said Amma. "I'm sorry, Sona."

"I think it's great Sona is standing in an election," said Appa. "It's OK to feel a bit nervous right now. Once the results are out, you'll go back to normal."

"But ..." said Thatha, "is it making her happy?"

No one said anything for a moment.

"Sometimes we *think* we want something," said Thatha, "but if we are sad while trying to get it and sad after we get it, why do we even want it?"

"Like the time you bought a car and didn't like to clean it or drive it," said Paatti.

"Yes," said Thatha. "That's why I sold it."

"Don't you want me to win the election, Thatha?" asked Sona.

"That's not what I'm saying, my almond moon," said Thatha. "I'm asking you if you're giving up the happiness in your heart and your friendship with Joy and Renu just to win?"

Oh! Sona hadn't thought about it like that.

Thatha's "On Time Every Time" pendulum clock rang five times.

"Look at the time!" said the President, placing Minmini back in the playpen. "I have to go and invite a few more people to the ceremony. See you all tomorrow. Sona, don't worry; be happy!"

The meeting was over. Everyone got on with their jobs.

Sona sat with Elephant on the sofa, watching Minmini.

"Bbb–bbbuuu..." called Minmini.

Sona kneeled in front of the playpen and reached out to her baby sister.

"If I were a real elephant," said Elephant, "I could cheer us all up by splashing water on everyone. That'd be fun."

"But I've never done anything without Joy and Renu," said Sona. "It's not fun without them. This whole week hasn't been fun."

"Sometimes you have to do things for others, even if it's not fun," said Elephant. "Like when Appa changes Minmini's nappies even when they're really stinky."

Sona giggled. "Maybe," she said. "I've got so much to do for the election too."

"Like what?" asked Elephant.

"I have to make a poster for the election period tomorrow," she said. "And then I have to prepare for my speech on Friday."

"Like Thatha says – one thing at a time, everything done in no time."

Back in her room, Elephant watched happily as Sona made her election poster. "You're surely going to win," he said. "Because your election symbol is me."

GATHERING VOTES

It was Thursday last period, which was reserved for what Miss Rao called "electioneering". Everyone's posters were up on the wall.

Sona put up her Elephant poster and wondered if she too should have come up with a slogan.

"Now you're allowed to talk to your classmates on their own or in groups," said Miss Rao.

"You should vote for me," said Sona to a group of girls at the front. "It's the only way to stop Pradeep winning."

Some of the girls nodded. Others didn't say anything.

Sona stole glances at Joy and Pradeep from time to time. Joy was talking earnestly to some classmates with a notebook in her hand, Renu by her side. Pradeep was sitting on a table, talking to a group of boys and girls.

The entire class was noisy because everyone was talking at the same time.

When Sona approached another group of classmates, they didn't smile at her, like they usually did.

"Hello!" started Sona, suddenly unsure of what to say.

"Hi, Sona," said one of the girls. "We're all voting for Joy."

"Why?" asked Sona.

"Because she has a plan for how to keep the classroom clean," said one of the boys.

"And she's always helpful," said another.

"And remember the Science project we did last term?" said one of the girls. "She was our leader, wasn't she?"

They all thought Joy would make a better class leader than Sona. But maybe she could be *more fun* than Joy, thought Sona.

"But we had a lot of fun during the Eco Dance that I organized, right?" said Sona. "The one we did during Eco Week?"

"Joy wrote the song for that, remember?" said Renu as she passed behind them.

Sona sat back in her seat. She wasn't really good at electioneering. Pradeep was talking and joking. Joy had a plan for what she would do when she became leader. All Sona had was "Vote for me, so Pradeep won't win!"

The period was still not over. Sona went up to talk to another group of classmates in the far corner of the classroom.

"Will you vote for me?" she asked.

"Maybe," said one of the girls.

Oh! Sona didn't know what to say.

"Will you be voting for Joy?" asked Sona.

"We don't know," said one of the boys.

"You and Joy are friends. If we vote for you,

Joy will get upset with us. If we vote for her, you might get upset."

Oh!

"We might vote for Pradeep," said another boy. "That way we can be friends with both of you."

Uh-oh! That was exactly what she had been afraid of. It was just like the story: the cat would eat the appam because the mice couldn't agree. *This is a disaster*, thought Sona.

But she had one final chance. She'd give a

really good speech tomorrow and convince them all to vote for her.

That evening, after school, Joy and Renu wouldn't talk to Sona in the auto-rickshaw. They talked only to each other, very loudly and deliberately about the election, and how everyone had promised to vote for Joy.

Sona tried to distract herself by counting the number of red cars they passed. After Joy and Renu had been dropped off, Mullai didn't head to Sona's house. She turned the auto-rickshaw towards The Orange, where the President lived.

"Your amma asked me to drop you off at the President's," she said. "Everyone in your house has gone out to do last-minute things for the ceremony."

"OK," said Sona sadly. All she wanted was to go home and talk to Elephant. Instead, she'd be stuck with the President, who would probably tell her off for not trying harder to win.

"The President has won many elections," said Mullai, as she brought the auto-rickshaw to a stop. "She'll have some amazing ideas for your speech."

Oh! Sona hadn't thought of that. Sona cheered up a little and decided to ask the President for help.

THE PRESIDENT'S COUNSEL

When the President opened the door, holding Elephant, Sona was cheered up a lot more.

"Hey, Sona!" she said. "Elephant wanted to stay with you until your amma comes to get you."

"Thanks!" said Sona, to the President and Elephant.

As Sona cuddled up with Elephant on the
sofa, the President asked, "What flavour
cupcakes would you like for the kids' party?"

"What kids' party?" said Sona.

"I thought you were planning one for
Minmini's celebration with all the kids," said
the President. "Or is it a show?"

Sona shook her head sadly. She hadn't
planned anything for Minmini. She wasn't
being a good big sister at all. The election was
messing everything up.

"Election troubles?" asked the President.

Sona shrugged.

"Why don't you tell me what's bothering you about the elections?" asked the President. "I've been a candidate many times."

"Did you win every time?"

"Sometimes I lost," said the President.

Sona said, "This is my first one and I want to win."

"And...?"

"But I don't know how," wailed Sona. "Pradeep will get votes because he makes the boys laugh. Many of our friends will vote for Joy because she has real plans about what she'll do when she becomes class leader. But..."

"Why should they elect you?" the President asked.

"I don't know," said Sona. "I just stood up to stop Pradeep from becoming class leader."

"Oh!" said the President.

Sona burst into tears. "I'm going to lose, aren't I?" she sobbed. "And whether I win or lose, I don't think Joy will ever talk to me again."

"Sona, you don't have to do anything if you don't want to do it," said the President. "If you want to drop out, then drop out."

"But ... I don't want to drop out!" yelled Sona.

The President reached for a notepad and a pencil on the table. "When I'm not sure about something I want to do," she said, "I always make a list of pros and cons."

The President drew a line down the middle of the blank page.

"This side is the pros – the good things about becoming class leader," she said. "This side is the cons – the not-so-good things about becoming class leader."

Handing the notepad and pencil to Sona, the

President said, "Let me get something for you to eat while you write down the pros and cons."

When Mullai had said the President had won lots of elections, Sona had assumed she'd help Sona win. But now the President was asking if she even *wanted* to win. Thatha had asked her if the election was making her happy. But of course she wanted to win, even if it made her sad.

"Make the list," nudged Elephant. "Maybe it'll help."

Sona wasn't sure how a list could help her, but no one argued with the President. She scribbled a few cons quite quickly. Then she thought about the pros for a long while. When she'd finished, Elephant gasped.

"You have more cons!" remarked Elephant.

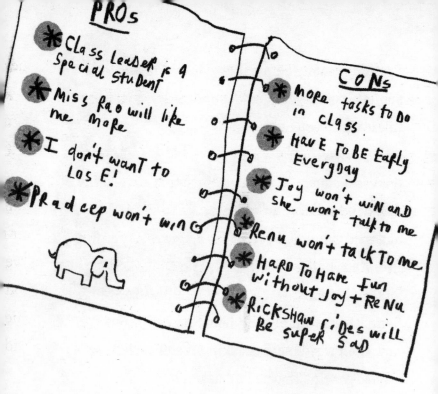

Tears fell from Sona's eyes.

The President bustled in carrying a plate of vegetable cutlets with ketchup. As Sona ate, the President told her about how she won the election to become the President of the college.

"I had many friends who helped me," she said. "No one can become a leader on their own."

"Hmmm," said Sona. "That's what I told Joy – that she should help me."

"Right," said the President.

Even when Amma came to pick Sona up, the President hadn't asked her about the pros and cons. And that was fine by Sona.

That night, when Sona was getting ready for bed, she showed the pros and cons sheet to Minmini.

"Look, Minmini," she said. "Lots of cons on my list."

"Mmm!" said Minmini.

"What should I do?" asked Sona.

Minmini didn't know. Neither did Elephant.

ELECTION DAY

Next morning, Sona got up earlier than usual.
It was Friday – Election Day. She started jotting
down ideas for a speech in her notebook.

"Do you have slogans too?" asked Elephant.

Good idea! Maybe she'd make up some
slogans with alliteration.

"Support Sona Sharma," she wrote.

Then she scratched it out. "I'll try a rhyme: North, south, east, west, Sona is the very best."

When she came down for breakfast, Thatha called out, "Here comes the new class leader!"

Sona looked up at him sadly. "Not yet, Thatha," she said.

"I give you my blessings," said Thatha, "that you will get what you want."

But what *did* she want? wondered Sona.

Patti touched Sona's head gently and said, "Do what's best for Sona. Whatever makes you happy."

But what *did* make her happy? wondered Sona again.

Amma and Appa came and sat next to her with their plates.

"Don't look so glum," said Appa. "Today is your big day, Sona. The election!"

"Whatever happens, you're still the same Sona," said Amma. "Elections will come and go. Go with the flow."

Appa groaned at Amma's rhyming advice. Sona smiled a little. Her family always cheered her up, even on the worst day ever, like Election Day.

DING-DONG!

A courier dropped off a parcel for Minmini from Aunty Lini in London.

"Oh, wow!" said Amma. "A wooden building set. I think Aunty Lini wants Minmini to become an engineer."

"Then I'll get her a coding kit as a present," said Appa.

"Don't be silly," said Amma. "She's too young for that."

"What did you get her?" asked Elephant.

"I forgot," whispered Sona. "I didn't get Minmini anything for her first birthday. I'm the worst sister ever! It's all because of the election."

"You've got a whole day," said Elephant.

"You can still get her something."

"But what?"

"Ask Minmini what she wants," said Elephant.

"But she can't talk," said Sona.

"She can pick," said Elephant. "Just like I can pick bananas from the tree."

Sona hugged Elephant. "That's a brilliant idea," she said.

But there was no time to do it right then. It was time for school and it was a big day. Sona had to give a convincing speech in the first period – she had an election to win!

※

The entire class was excited. Miss Rao asked Sona, Joy and Pradeep to sit facing the class. Miss Rao chose the order of speakers by drawing lots: Pradeep was to go first, Joy second and Sona last. Sona had wanted to get her speech over with as soon as possible, but now she was stuck in the chair until Pradeep and Joy finished theirs.

Miss Rao put up another poster. This time it said, "RULES FOR SPEECHES".

RULES FOR SPEECHES

1. You can speak for 5 minutes.

2. Do not be rude.

3. Do not make promises you can't keep.

"Good luck, Pradeep, Joy and Sona," said Miss Rao with a smile. "May the best candidate win."

Everyone started talking all at once.

Miss Rao clapped her hands. "Right! Pradeep, if you're ready?" she said, turning on the timer.

Pradeep got up and grinned at everyone. He spent the first minute just waving to his friends and pulling funny faces, making everyone laugh.

"Do you have a speech?" asked Miss Rao.

"If I become class leader," he began, "I'll do magic tricks during breaks and make up jokes."

Some of his friends groaned.

"Wait!" said Pradeep. "I also want to set up break-time Olympics between all the classes on our floor."

BUZZ!

The timer buzzed and Pradeep sat back in his chair. Everyone clapped. Sona thought break-time Olympics was a great idea.

Then it was Joy's turn. She smiled at everyone and began: "If I become class leader, I'll aim to win the Tidiest Class prize this year."

Some boys groaned.

"I also want to start a nature club in our class,"

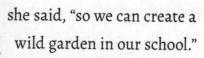

she said, "so we can create a wild garden in our school."

Many cheered.

"And I'll help Pradeep to organize the break-time Olympics too," finished Joy.

Everyone clapped. Miss Rao laughed loudly as she pressed the buzzer.

It was Sona's turn now. She opened her notebook at the speech points and slogans she had written. But another sheet of paper fell out – her pros and cons list. Sona stared at the sheet as if it was growing into a paper monster right before her eyes.

"Sona, whenever you're ready," said Miss Rao. That meant Sona had to hurry up.

Sona looked up at the class and smiled.

"Good morning!" she shouted.

"Inside voice, Sona," said Miss Rao.

Sona's legs shook. She tried to stare at the wall at the far end of the classroom.

"Pradeep's ideas were fun," she said. "But Joy wants to do more. She wants our class to win prizes, learn new skills and have fun."

Some cheered and some giggled.

"We know," shouted Renu.

"Shh," warned Miss Rao.

"I ... I..." Sona hesitated, looking down at the sheets of paper in her hand. Then she took a deep breath and looked at her friends.

"I want you all to vote for Joy!" said Sona.

Everyone gasped.

Renu shouted, "WHAT?"

"I want you all to vote for Joy, because then we can learn together at nature club, win the Tidiest Class prize *and* have break-time Olympics, all at the same time."

Miss Rao clapped her hands to quieten the class. "Sona!" she said. "Are you...?"

"I don't want to be class leader, Miss," replied Sona. "I want Joy to be our class leader."

Everyone clapped and cheered.

Pradeep scowled at Sona as she returned to her seat.

"This has changed things," said Miss Rao. "But even in real elections, people do drop out and endorse other candidates."

"What is 'endorse', Miss?" asked Renu.

"'Endorse' means supporting another candidate instead of yourself."

"Thanks for endorsing Joy," shouted Renu with a big grin.

Sona smiled. For the first time that week, Renu had smiled at her. Joy reached over and twined her fingers into Sona's.

"Right, class," said Miss Rao. "We've heard from the candidates. After the break, we will prepare for the election."

While the rest of the class ran to get their snacks and water, Sona and Joy were still sitting next to each other. Joy leaned closer to Sona and whispered, "Thank you! You're the best."

"I'm sorry I didn't check with you before I became a candidate," said Sona.

"Sorry I was rude to you," said Joy. "I should have told you that I'd been dreaming about becoming class leader since last year. My older sister was a class leader too."

Renu ran up to Sona and Joy and they hugged each other and jumped together. For a long time.

"I'm sorry too," said Renu. "Maybe I shouldn't have taken sides."

"Why did you change your mind?" asked Joy.

"Because of this," said Sona, showing her the pros and cons list. "There were more cons than pros! See!"

And that was that. Sona had done what made her happy. Being a good friend. Not fighting with her best friends. And definitely not becoming class leader.

"You're coming tomorrow, right?" asked Sona. "For Minmini's birthday?"

"Yes!" said Joy and Renu.

"Do you want to do a show for all the kids who come to the ceremony?" asked Sona.

"Like a musical?" asked Renu. Renu loved musicals.

"I haven't decided," said Sona.

"Then we both will come to your house early tomorrow," said Joy. "We'll decide, plan and do the show!"

"The class leader is taking charge," teased Sona.

They all laughed.

※

The class spent the rest of the morning getting ready for the election.

Some made ballot boxes. Others rearranged tables to create voting booths.

Sona was in charge of making ballot papers with Joy and Pradeep's symbols on them. With Renu's help, Sona made the thirty ballots in no time at all.

Voting began right after lunch. There were two queues in front of two "voting booths". Each booth had a ballot box.

Each person went up to the booth and collected a ballot paper. They ticked against the candidate name they were voting for. Then they folded the ballot paper and dropped it into the box.

They weren't allowed to tell anyone who they had voted for.

"Voting is anonymous," reminded Miss Rao. "And don't tick both the boxes, because then your vote will *not* be counted."

Joy and Pradeep were allowed to vote too.

"Who did you vote for?" Renu asked Joy.

"Guess who!" said Joy, laughing. "My mum said I'd at least get one vote."

"You'll at least get three votes for sure," said Sona.

Voting took almost all afternoon, even though there were just thirty of them in the class. After all of them had voted, Miss Rao collected the ballot boxes and locked them away in the store cupboard. By the time they had returned the classroom back to its normal state, the school day was over.

"Miss, who won the election?" asked Pradeep.

"You'll find out on Monday," said Miss Rao. "We're going to have a lesson on counting votes, too."

That evening, when they ran to the auto-rickshaw, Mullai figured it out straight away. "This is a miracle! You three are best friends again!"

"Yeah!" said Sona. "For ever and ever."

"That's great," said Mullai. "How did that happen?"

"I dropped out of the election and ..." started Sona.

"... and she *endorsed* me," finished Joy. "Sona is the best."

"I did not see that coming," said Mullai.

"But I'm so happy that you're all friends again."

"Whether I win or Pradeep wins," said Joy, "we three will always be best friends. Agreed?"

"So, it's all agreed that we're friends indeed," said Sona.

Renu groaned and teased, "Still rhyming slogans?"

Sona hugged Joy and Renu and said, "Tomorrow, we'll plan a birthday show for Minmini!"

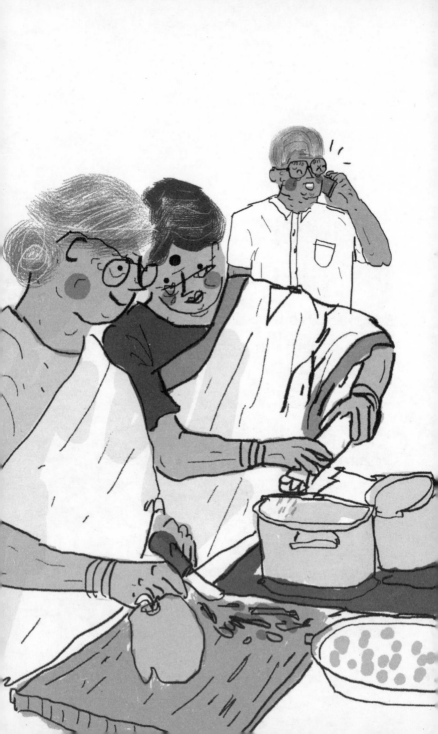

BiRTHDaY
CELEBRATiONS

Everyone was busy as bees on Saturday morning. Paatti was in charge of the food with the President's help. Thatha was in charge of everything to do with the motorbike priest.

Appa had to get Minmini ready. Amma was up early, so she could receive the guests and take them to the roof terrace, where the ceremony was taking place. A pandhal had been erected, just like they'd had for Minmini's naming ceremony. And the motorbike priest was expected any time.

Sona, Joy and Renu started early to plan their show. "Should we do a dance or should we sing?" asked Renu.

"How about a play?" said Joy.

Sona's eyes lit up. "I already have the script for 'The Two Mice and the Cat'."

"Who is going to be the cat?" asked Joy.

"Me!" shouted Renu. "You two are the mice who fought and then finally worked it out. I'm the cat who will eat all the appam!"

She made a chomp-chomp face and they all giggled.

Joy created a to-do list, which was a very good thing, because there was a lot to do.

minmini's BIRthDAY SHOW

- make cat + mice masks
- Learn the Lines
- make signs for the stage
- make the stage
- make props for the Appam
- Find someone to video the show

They got busy and soon Joy had ticked off all the items on the list except the last one.

Elephant lay back on the bed and watched them laugh and chat. He was happy that Sona was happy.

Soon it was time for the ceremony. Paatti helped Sona, Joy and Renu get ready – they put on silk skirts and blouses, and plaited their hair with matching ribbons and jasmine flower strings.

"You look like three goddesses," she said. "Come on up quickly, the motorbike priest will be here any minute."

Amma sat next to Appa on his right, with Minmini on her lap. The priest sat on Appa's left and quietly told him what to do. In front of them, bricks were arranged to form a square. Inside that, the priest had built a fire from sticks and dried grass.

Every time Appa chanted and added some ghee into the fire, smoke rose into the air and Minmini cried. Amma's eyes were watering too.

The guests were sitting across from Amma

and Appa, on the other side of the fire. Everyone
had a handkerchief to wipe away the tears
caused by the smoke.

"Too much smoke," said Appa.

"We need the god of fire as a witness to our
prayers," said the priest, adding more ghee to
the fire. "We need his blessings for the baby."

Sona, Joy and Renu sat behind Amma,
distracting Minmini. But, as the breeze picked
up, the smoke irritated their eyes too.

"Maybe we should start our show now?" suggested Sona.

"Good idea," whispered Amma. "Have you got everything?"

Joy nodded. They had put up the signs to the garden, where they were doing the show. They had the props. They had the masks.

"We just need someone to video us," said Joy.

"I'll do it," said Mullai, from across the room. "I can't wait to get away from the smoke."

Sona, Joy and Renu ran ahead to the garden, where they had drawn a square on the mud using rice flour to show that it was the stage.

Mullai came down, bringing all the kids with her, along with some adults holding their babies. Mullai pulled out her phone ready to record.

Sona banged on a steel tumbler with a

big ladle to get everyone's attention. Then Joy came to the front and said, "SJR Productions presents … 'The Two Mice and the Greedy Cat'."

The three of them put their masks on and the show began.

The two mice pretended to fight over a very big appam, which was actually a sofa cushion.

Renu jumped up on stage as the cat, making everyone laugh. She made funny mewling sounds as she pretended to munch on the appam.

The audience howled with laughter.

When they had finished the show, Sona, Joy and Renu removed their masks and took a bow just like they did after their school plays.

Everyone clapped, and some of the little ones crawled about, pretending to be the cat eating the appam.

"Did you video all of it?" Sona asked Mullai. "I want to show it to everyone later."

"Ooops! Sorry," said Mullai. "The show was so good that I forgot to record it."

"Oh no!" shouted Renu.

"Mullai's joking," said Joy. "Aren't you?"

By the time they went upstairs, the ceremony had finished and the grown-ups were chatting.

"Where's Minmini?" asked Sona.

"Downstairs with Paatti," said Amma.

Sona picked up her box of toys and took it downstairs to Minmini, who was playing on the floor in the living room.

"Happy birthday, Minmini!" they all shouted together.

Minmini looked up and clapped her hands.

"Are all these toys for Minmini?" asked Joy.

"I want her to choose whatever she wants," said Sona. She held up a dragon first. Then a rhino.

Under the toys was a magic wand. Joy picked it up and asked, "Sona, if you could make a wish for Minmini, what would it be?"

"That she'll get good friends, just like I have you two," said Sona.

"And me, three," said Elephant.

"Don't give the magic wand to the baby, sweetie," said Paatti, as she walked past. "It's not safe."

"Look, the dinosaur," said Renu. "We used to play with it in the nursery."

But Minmini didn't want any of the toys. She swatted them all away.

"Try that," said Elephant to Sona. Sona picked up Serpo, the cuddly red squirrel that Uncle Prasad had brought her from Scotland.

"Here's Serpo, little sister," said Sona.

Minmini reached out. Then she pulled it from Sona's hands.

"Yay! She likes Serpo," said Sona.

"Well, Serpo was one of your favourites when you were little," said Elephant. "Your *second* favourite, of course."

Then it was time for lunch and, after lunch, Sona, Joy and Renu played together all afternoon.

That night, as Sona lay in bed, she smiled brightly like the moon in the sky. She was happy that she had remembered how to be a good friend, just in time.

"Sona Sharma – you're a good friend indeed," said Elephant.

"Thanks," said Sona.

"I have one question, though," said Elephant.

"Hmm?"

"How come that red squirrel is called Serpo and I don't have a name at all?"

But Sona didn't reply. She was fast asleep, dreaming happy dreams.

CLASS LEADER
INAUGURATION

It was Monday morning. It was the day they'd
find out who had won the election.

"Tell Joy I wished her good luck," said Amma,
as she waved Sona off in Mullai's auto-rickshaw.

Joy was quiet when they collected her, but
Renu was just as excited as Sona.

"You'll win," said Sona. "For sure."

"I'm not so sure," said Joy.

"Good luck, girls," shouted Mullai, when she dropped them off at school.

The bell rang and it was time for class to start. After taking the register (and that day it was names of trees), Miss Rao opened her Maths book as if she had forgotten all about the election.

"Miss!" Sona called, with her hand up.

"Yes, Sona?" said Miss Rao.

"Have you counted the votes?"

"What votes?"

Everyone gasped.

"The election votes," shouted Pradeep.

Miss Rao laughed. "I'm only joking," she said. "I need counting volunteers, one for each candidate."

Joy huddled with Sona and Renu. "You go, Sona," said Renu. "I'll stay with Joy. You can add up faster than me."

"I hope I get it right," said Sona, walking up to Miss Rao.